AF373637

Rising Tide: The Rebirth of Ramsey

The Impact Chronicles, Volume 3

Paul Smith

Published by Paul Smith, 2024.

RISING TIDE: THE REBIRTH OF RAMSEY

First edition. February 23, 2024.

Copyright © 2024 Paul Smith.

ISBN: 979-8224475711

Written by Paul Smith.

Table of Contents

In dedication to my late father Malcolm Smith, 48-2020 Always dare to dream, Keep going - only you can do it mate, becasue its a big world out there.

In Book 3, " Rising Tide: The Rebirth of Ramsey," Ramsey faces a new challenge when a devastating storm tests the town's resilience. As old wounds resurface and tensions rise, the residents must confront the shadows of the past and find the courage to rebuild and heal together, forging stronger bonds and deeper connections

in the process.

Synopsis:

"The Impact Chronicles" is a series of interconnected stories that illuminate the resilience, compassion, and transformative power of individuals and communities facing adversity. Set in the coastal town of Ramsey, each instalment follows the journey of diverse characters as they navigate personal struggles, overcome obstacles, and unite to create positive change. From rebuilding after natural disasters to fostering community connections, these tales inspire hope, resilience, and the belief that even the smallest actions can make a big difference.

Now, let's dive in.

Title: Rising Tide: The Rebirth of Ramsey

Summary:
In "Rising Tide: The Rebirth of Ramsey," the third instalment of the "Impact Chronicles" series, we witness the resilience and strength of the coastal town of Ramsey in the aftermath of a devastating storm.

Chapter 1: Aftermath

In the morning aftermath of the devastating storm, Ramsey lay in shambles and shaken. Debris littered the streets, buildings lay in ruins, and the once bustling town was now a grey cold shadow of its former self.

Adam and Emily emerged from their shelter to survey the damage, their hearts heavy with grief for their community.

As they walked through the wreckage, they were met with scenes of devastation. Homes destroyed, businesses in ruins, and families displaced. It was a sobering reminder of the power of nature and the fragility of human existence.

But amidst the destruction, there were signs of hope. Neighbours emerged from their homes to lend a hand, volunteers arrived to offer support, and the spirit of resilience began to stir within the community. Adam and Emily knew that rebuilding would be a long and arduous journey, but they were determined to see their town rise from the ashes stronger than ever before.

Chapter 2: Assessing the Damage

With the initial shock of the storm beginning to subside, Adam and Emily, along with other community members, set out to assess the full extent of the damage inflicted upon Ramsey.

They walked through the town, taking note of every broken window, collapsed roof, and

flooded street. It was a daunting task, and with each new sight of destruction, their resolve was tested.

As they surveyed the damage, they encountered stories of loss and resilience from their

fellow townspeople. Some had lost their homes entirely, while others had miraculously

escaped unscathed. But despite the differences in their experiences, they all shared a common determination to rebuild and restore their beloved town.

By the end of the day, Adam and Emily had compiled a comprehensive list of the town's

needs and priorities. It was clear that the road ahead would be long and challenging, but they

were ready to roll up their sleeves and get to work, one step at a time.

Chapter 3: Rallying Together

As news of the storm's devastation spread throughout Ramsey, the community began to rally together in a display of solidarity and resilience.

Adam and Emily found themselves at the forefront of the effort, organising meetings and community gatherings to coordinate the town's response to the crisis. They were joined by friends, neighbours, and local leaders, all eager to lend a hand and offer support however they could.

Together, they devised a plan of action, dividing tasks and responsibilities among different groups and individuals. Some focused on clearing debris and repairing infrastructure, while others worked to provide aid and assistance to those in need.

The sense of unity and purpose that emerged from these collective efforts was palpable. Despite the challenges that lay ahead, the people of Ramsey stood shoulder to shoulder, determined to rebuild their town and restore hope to their community.

Chapter 4: Rebuilding Plans

With the initial stages of cleanup underway and the community rallied together, Adam and Emily convened a meeting to discuss the next steps in Ramsey's rebuilding efforts.

Gathered in the town hall, residents shared their ideas and concerns as they looked towards the future. Together, they began to outline a comprehensive plan for rebuilding Ramsey, taking into account the town's unique needs and priorities.

Key areas of focus emerged during the meeting, including the restoration of essential

infrastructure, the revitalization of local businesses, and the creation of safe and resilient housing for those displaced by the storm.

Adam and Emily offered their expertise and resources to support these efforts, pledging to use their shop and gallery, Renewal, as a hub for community organising and support.

By the end of the meeting, a sense of optimism and determination permeated the room.

Despite the challenges that lay ahead, the people of Ramsey were united in their commitment to rebuilding their town and creating a brighter future for all who called it home.

Chapter 5: A Community United

In the wake of the storm's devastation, the people of Ramsey found strength and resilience in

their unity.

Neighbours helped neighbours, strangers became friends, and the bonds of community grew

stronger than ever before. Together, they worked tirelessly to clear debris, repair damage,

and support those in need.

Volunteers poured in from neighbouring towns, offering their assistance and expertise in the

rebuilding efforts. The spirit of generosity and compassion was contagious, spreading

throughout the community like wildfire.

As they worked side by side, the people of Ramsey discovered a renewed sense of purpose

and belonging. They realised that together, they were capable of overcoming any obstacle

and rebuilding their town stronger and more resilient than ever before.

United in their determination, they forged ahead, confident in their ability to rise above

adversity and create a brighter future for themselves and future generations.

Chapter 6: Clearing the Debris

With the community united and spirits high, the daunting task of clearing the debris from

Ramsey's streets began in earnest.

Volunteers armed with shovels, brooms, and wheelbarrows descended upon the town,

working tirelessly to remove fallen trees, broken branches, and other debris left in the storm's

wake.

It was slow and exhausting work, but the sense of camaraderie and shared purpose kept

morale high. Neighbours helped neighbours out as they cleared away the remnants of the storm, offering encouragement and support along the way.

As the days passed and the streets began to clear, a sense of progress and accomplishment

filled the air. The community had come together in a remarkable display of resilience, proving

that even in the face of adversity, they were stronger together than they could ever be alone.

Chapter 7: Seeds of Hope

Amidst the rubble and destruction, seeds of hope began to sprout in the hearts of Ramsey's residents.

Adam and Emily, along with other community leaders, worked tirelessly to inspire optimism and positivity in the face of adversity. They organised community meetings and events, sharing stories of resilience and determination to uplift spirits and foster a sense of hope for the future.

Volunteers planted flowers and trees in the newly cleared areas, symbolising new beginnings and growth amidst the devastation. Each bloom served as a reminder that even in the darkest of times, there is always the potential for beauty and renewal.

As the days passed, these seeds of hope took root and began to flourish, spreading throughout the community like wildfire. People found strength in each other, drawing inspiration from the resilience and determination of their neighbours.

Though the road ahead was long and challenging, the seeds of hope planted in Ramsey's soil promised a brighter tomorrow for all who called it home.

Chapter 8: Planning for the Future

With the initial cleanup efforts well underway and a renewed sense of hope permeating the
community, Adam, Emily, and other town leaders began to turn their attention towards
planning for Ramsey's future.

Gathered in the town hall once again, they discussed long-term strategies for rebuilding and
revitalising the town. Ideas were exchanged, proposals were debated, and priorities were
identified to guide the community's efforts in the months and years to come.

Key areas of focus included:

Infrastructure: Plans were made to repair and upgrade essential infrastructure such
as roads, bridges, and utilities to ensure the town's resilience in the face of future
storms.

Economic Development: Strategies were developed to support local businesses and
attract new investment to stimulate economic growth and create jobs for residents.

Housing: Efforts were made to provide affordable and resilient housing options for
those displaced by the storm, ensuring that everyone had a safe and stable place to

call home.

Community Resilience: Initiatives were launched to strengthen the community's

resilience to future disasters, including education and outreach programs, emergency

preparedness efforts, and environmental conservation initiatives.

As they worked together to shape Ramsey's future, Adam, Emily, and their fellow community

members were filled with a sense of optimism and determination. They knew that the road

ahead would be challenging, but they were confident that by planning thoughtfully and

working together, they could create a stronger, more vibrant Ramsey for generations to

Come. Keeping its own younger generations for longer.

Chapter 9: Breaking Ground

With plans in place and the community's vision for the future clear, it was time to take the

first tangible steps towards rebuilding Ramsey.

Amidst a sense of anticipation and excitement, Adam, Emily, and a team of volunteers

gathered at the site of the town's first major reconstruction project. Armed with shovels, hard

hats, and a shared sense of purpose, they broke ground on the construction site, marking the

beginning of a new chapter in Ramsey's history.

As the first piles of earth were turned over, a feeling of hope and determination swept

through the crowd. This moment symbolised not just the physical rebuilding of the town, but

also the resilience and strength of its people in the face of adversity.

With each swing of the shovel and each load of dirt moved, Ramsey moved one step closer

to realise its vision of a brighter, more prosperous future. And as the sun set on the first

day of construction, a sense of optimism filled the air, setting the stage for the

transformational journey that lay ahead.

Chapter 10: Building Back Better

As construction progressed in Ramsey, the community embraced the opportunity to not just

rebuild, but to build back better than before.

Adam, Emily, and their fellow residents worked closely with architects, engineers, and

construction crews to ensure that new buildings and infrastructure were designed with

resilience and sustainability in mind. From reinforced structures to eco-friendly materials,

every detail was carefully considered to withstand future challenges and minimise

environmental impact.

The town's new buildings rose from the rubble, each one a testament to the community's

determination to create a more resilient and vibrant Ramsey. From affordable housing

developments to modernised business districts, the town began to take shape in a way that

reflected the hopes and dreams of its residents.

As they watched their town transform before their eyes, Adam and Emily felt a sense of pride

and accomplishment. Though the journey had been difficult, they knew that the challenges

they had faced had only made them stronger, and that together, they had laid the foundation for a brighter future for Ramsey and all who called it home.

Chapter 11: Overcoming Setbacks

Despite the progress made in rebuilding Ramsey, the community encountered setbacks
along the way.

Delays in construction, unforeseen logistical challenges, and financial hurdles threatened to
derail the town's recovery efforts. Adam, Emily, and their fellow residents faced moments of
frustration and disappointment as they grappled with these obstacles.

However, rather than succumbing to despair, the community rallied together once again,
drawing strength from their shared determination to overcome adversity. They adapted their
plans, sought creative solutions to their problems, and leaned on each other for support.

Through perseverance and resilience, they found ways to navigate the challenges they faced,
emerging stronger and more united than before. Each setback became an opportunity for
growth and learning, reinforcing their commitment to rebuilding Ramsey and creating a
better future for all.

Chapter 12: A New Vision

As Ramsey's reconstruction progressed and setbacks were overcome, Adam, Emily, and their

fellow community members began to envision a new future for their town.

Inspired by the resilience and creativity they had witnessed throughout the rebuilding

process, they dared to dream of a Ramsey that was not just restored to its former glory, but

transformed into a beacon of innovation and sustainability.

Gathered in town hall meetings and community workshops, they shared ideas and

aspirations for the future. From green infrastructure projects to community gardens,

renewable energy initiatives to local economic development programs, the possibilities

seemed endless.

With a renewed sense of purpose and determination, Adam, Emily, and their neighbours set

out to turn these visions into reality. They knew that creating lasting change would require

hard work, collaboration, and unwavering commitment, but they were undeterred.

Together, they embarked on a journey to build a future for Ramsey that was resilient, inclusive, and vibrant—a future that honoured the past while embracing the opportunities of

tomorrow. And as they looked ahead, they knew that with determination and perseverance,

anything was possible.

Chapter 13: The Spirit of Ramsey

As the reconstruction efforts in Ramsey continued, a remarkable spirit emerged within the
community—a spirit of resilience, unity, and hope.

Neighbours helped neighbours rebuild their homes, businesses offered support to one another,
and volunteers from near and far lent their time and resources to the recovery efforts. In
every corner of the town, people came together in a display of solidarity and compassion
that was truly inspiring to witness.

But it wasn't just the physical rebuilding of Ramsey that demonstrated this spirit—it was the
way that people supported each other emotionally and spiritually as well. Whether through a
kind word, a helping hand, or a shared meal, the people of Ramsey showed that they were
there for each other in good times and bad.

This spirit of Ramsey became a source of strength and resilience for the community as they
faced the challenges of rebuilding. It reminded them that they were not alone, and that
together, they could overcome any obstacle that stood in their way.

As the days turned into weeks and the weeks into months, the spirit of Ramsey only grew stronger, serving as a beacon of hope and inspiration for all who called the town home. And

as the town continued to rebuild and recover, this spirit would remain at the heart of

everything they did, guiding them forward into a brighter future.

Chapter 14: Rising from the Ashes

Like a phoenix emerging from the ashes, Ramsey began to rise anew from the devastation

left by the storm.

With each passing day, signs of progress became more evident. New buildings replaced

those that had been destroyed, streets were repaved, and parks were revitalised. The town

was slowly but surely reclaiming its former beauty and vitality.

But it wasn't just the physical reconstruction that marked Ramsey's rebirth—it was the

resilience and determination of its people. The community had come together in a

remarkable display of solidarity, working hand in hand to rebuild their town and support one

another along the way.

As they looked around at the progress they had made, Adam, Emily, and their fellow

residents felt a sense of pride and optimism. Though the road ahead would undoubtedly be

challenging, they knew that together, they were capable of overcoming any obstacle.

With each new building, each new park, and each new opportunity, Ramsey was rising from

the ashes are stronger and more resilient than ever before. And as the town continued to rebuild

and recover, its spirit would serve as a testament to the power of community and the triumph
of hope over adversity.

Chapter 15: Strengthening Bonds

Amidst the process of rebuilding Ramsey, the bonds between its residents grew deeper and

stronger than ever before.

Neighbours became like family, united by shared experiences and a common goal. They

leaned on each other for support, offering a listening ear, a helping hand, or a shoulder to

lean on in times of need.

Community events and gatherings became opportunities for connection and camaraderie.

Whether it was a neighbourhood barbecue, a town hall meeting, or a volunteer clean-up effort,

people came together to work towards a common purpose and strengthen the ties that

bound them.

As they worked side by side, Adam, Emily, and their fellow residents discovered a renewed

sense of belonging and community. They realised that the true strength of Ramsey lay not

just in its buildings and infrastructure, but in the connections between its people.

And as the town continued to rebuild and recover, these bonds would serve as the

foundation upon which a brighter, more resilient future would be built.

Chapter 16: Celebrating Progress

With each milestone reached in Ramsey's rebuilding efforts, the community came together
to celebrate the progress made and the resilience shown in the face of adversity.

Street parties, festivals, and community gatherings were organised to mark key moments in
the town's recovery journey. Residents and volunteers alike filled the streets, sharing stories,
laughter, and hope for the future.

Local businesses reopened their doors, welcoming customers old and new with open arms.

The sounds of music, laughter, and conversation filled the air once more, signalling a return
to normalcy and a renewed sense of vibrancy in the town.

As they celebrated how far they had come, Adam, Emily, and their fellow residents felt a
profound sense of gratitude and pride. They knew that the road ahead would still be
challenging, but they also knew that they had the strength, resilience, and support of their
community to see them through.

And as they looked ahead to the future, they did so with optimism and determination,
knowing that together, they could overcome any obstacle and build a brighter tomorrow for

Ramsey and all who called it home.

Chapter 17: Facing Challenges

Despite the progress made in rebuilding Ramsey, the community continued to face
challenges along the way.

New obstacles arose, from logistical hurdles to financial constraints, threatening to slow
down the town's recovery efforts. Adam, Emily, and their fellow residents found themselves
grappling with tough decisions and difficult circumstances, unsure of the best path forward.

Yet, in the face of adversity, the spirit of resilience that had come to define Ramsey remained
unwavering. People rallied together, offering support and encouragement to one another in small social gatherings in the old town hall, as they navigated through uncertain times.

Through their perseverance and determination, the community confronted each challenge the town council threw at them head-on, refusing to be deterred in their quest to rebuild and revitalise their town. As the towns public noticed this uprising and this drew strength from their shared commitment to the future of Ramsey, knowing that together, they could overcome whatever obstacles lay in their path. They just needed a way of voicing their concerns.

Chapter 18: Embracing Change

As Ramsey continued its journey of rebuilding and renewal, the community began to

embrace the changes that came with it.

People recognized that the town could not simply return to the way it was before the storm.

Instead, they saw an opportunity to reimagine Ramsey as a more resilient, inclusive, and

sustainable place to live.

Residents embraced new ideas and initiatives aimed at improving the town's infrastructure,

promoting economic growth, and enhancing quality of life for all. They welcomed innovation

and creativity, eager to explore new possibilities and seize opportunities for positive change.

Adam, Emily, and their fellow residents played an active role in driving this transformation,

contributing their talents, energy, and passion to the collective effort. Together, they worked

towards a shared vision of a brighter future for Ramsey—one that reflected the values and

aspirations of its diverse community.

As they embraced change, the people of Ramsey found strength in their resilience, unity, and

optimism. They understood that while change could be daunting, it also held the promise of a better tomorrow—a tomorrow that they were determined to shape together.

Chapter 19: Seeds of Renewal

As the rebuilding efforts in Ramsey continued, the community planted the seeds of renewal

that would pave the way for a brighter future.

New businesses emerged, bringing fresh energy and innovation to the town's economy. From

local artisans and entrepreneurs to tech startups and social enterprises, Ramsey became a

hub of creativity and entrepreneurship, attracting visitors from far and wide.

Community gardens flourished, providing fresh produce and green spaces for residents to

enjoy. Urban farming initiatives and sustainability projects took root, promoting

environmental stewardship and food security for generations to come.

But perhaps most importantly, the seeds of renewal were sown in the hearts and minds of

Ramsey's residents themselves. People embraced a spirit of resilience, optimism, and hope,

determined to build a community that was stronger, more inclusive, and more vibrant than

ever before.

As they worked together to nurture these seeds, Adam, Emily, and their fellow residents knew that the journey ahead would be challenging, but they also knew that they had the power to shape their own destiny. And with each passing day, Ramsey grew closer to

realising its full potential as a place of opportunity, creativity, and possibilities compared with the other towns regenerations.

Chapter 20: A Brighter Tomorrow

As Ramsey's journey of rebuilding and renewal drew to a close, the community looked ahead

to a brighter tomorrow filled with hope and possibility.

The town had overcome immense challenges and obstacles, emerging stronger, more

resilient, and more united than ever before. From the ashes of devastation had risen a new

Ramsey—one defined by innovation, creativity, and a deep sense of community.

New businesses thrived, breathing life into the town's economy and bringing renewed energy

to its streets. Parks and public spaces bustled with activity, as residents young and old came

together to enjoy the beauty of their revitalised surroundings.

But perhaps the greatest transformation of all was the one that had taken place within the

hearts and minds of Ramsey's residents. People had discovered a newfound sense of

purpose and belonging, recognizing the power of collective action and the importance of

working together towards common goals.

As they looked ahead to the future, Adam, Emily, and their fellow residents knew that

challenges would undoubtedly arise, but they also knew that they were better equipped than ever to face them head-on. With the spirit of resilience, optimism, and community that had

carried them through the darkest of times, they were ready to embrace whatever the future

held and continue building a town that they could be proud to call home.

Book 4, "Seeds of Renewal: Love's Everlasting Bloom,"

BOOK 4, "SEEDS OF RENEWAL: Love's Everlasting Bloom," shifts focus to Emily and

Adam as they navigate the complexities of love, loss, and renewal. Through their

journey, they discover that love has the power to heal wounds, ignite passions, and

inspire transformation, reminding them of the enduring hope that lies within each

new beginning.

Through its heartfelt narratives and compelling characters, "The Impact Chronicles"
explores the universal themes of compassion, resilience, and the profound impact of
small acts of kindness and courage. It serves as a testament to the indomitable human spirit and the infinite possibilities that arise when individuals come together to create positive change in the world.

Rising Tide: The Rebirth of Ramsey

The Impact Chronicles - Written by Paul Smith

Rising Tide: The Rebirth of Ramsey

The Impact Chronicles - Written by Paul Smith

Rising Tide: The Rebirth of Ramsey

The Impact Chronicles - Written by Paul Smith

Thank you
@woodystanks

Rising Tide: The Rebirth of Ramsey

The Impact Chronicles - Written by Paul Smith

Also by Paul Smith

The Impact Chronicles
Seeds of Change: A Journey to Ramsey
Roots of Resilience: Nurturing Change
Rising Tide: The Rebirth of Ramsey
Seeds of Renewal: Love's Everlasting Bloom
Journey to the Depths: Angels and Demons

Watch for more at wix.pbsmith17@wix.com.

About the Author

Paul smith Artist, Aurthor & Designer. Island resident since 1999 Read more at wix.pbsmith17@wix.com.